CW01497282

Granny's Ghost and the Haunted Homicide

Ghostly Gumshoe Cozy Mysteries Series, Volume 1

Sloane Finley

Published by Ginger and Spice Publishing, 2025.

This is a work of fiction. Similarities to real people, places, or events are entirely coincidental.

GRANNY'S GHOST AND THE HAUNTED HOMICIDE

First edition. June 28, 2025.

ISBN: 979-8231894192

Written by Sloane Finley.

Table of Contents

Chapter 1... 1

Chapter 2... 7

Chapter 3...13

Chapter 4...19

Chapter 5...25

Chapter 6...30

Chapter 7...35

Chapter 8...43

Chapter 9...48

Chapter 10 55

Chapter 11 62

Chapter 12 70

Chapter 1

I step off the bus, my suitcase wheels clattering on the cracked sidewalk of New Oslo's main street. The crisp autumn air carries a hint of woodsmoke, stirring memories I'd almost forgotten. It's been fifteen years since I last visited Grandma Ingrid, and now her Victorian house is mine.

"Well, if it ain't little Lena Larson!" A gruff voice calls out. I turn to see old Harold Peterson, looking exactly as I remember him—suspenders, plaid shirt, and all. "Though I guess you ain't so little anymore."

I force a smile. "Hi, Mr. Peterson. Nice to see some things haven't changed."

But as I make my way down the street, it's clear that plenty has. The general store where Grandma used to buy me candy is now a sleek coffee shop. The old movie theater's marquee advertises indie films instead of blockbusters. Even the town square feels different—the ancient oak tree is gone, replaced by a modern sculpture that looks like a tangle of metal pipes. It's obvious that the small town I remember has grown.

I pause at the corner, disoriented. The familiarity I'd expected eludes me, leaving me feeling like a stranger in a place I once called home.

"Lena? Is that you?"

I turn to see Charlene Bergstrom, my childhood best friend. Her blonde hair is shorter now, and there are laugh lines around her eyes that weren't there before.

"Charlie! I didn't know if you still lived here."

She pulls me into a hug. "Born and raised, remember? Some of us never left." There's a hint of something in her voice—envy? Resentment?—but it's gone before I can place it. "I heard about your grandma. I'm so sorry."

"Thanks," I murmur, suddenly aware of the house key weighing heavy in my pocket. "I'm actually heading there now. To the house, I mean."

Charlene's eyes widen. "You're keeping it?"

I shrug, uncomfortable under her scrutiny. "I'm not sure yet. I need to see it first, figure things out."

"Well, don't be a stranger," Charlene says, already backing away. "We should catch up while you're in town."

I nod, watching her go. The interaction leaves me unsettled, like trying to fit into clothes I've long outgrown.

As I round the corner onto Maple Street, Grandma Ingrid's house comes into view. The pale yellow paint is peeling, the wraparound porch sagging slightly. But the stained-glass window above the door still catches the late afternoon sun, sending prisms of color dancing across the overgrown lawn.

I take a deep breath, steeling myself. This house holds fifteen years of missed visits and unanswered calls. Fifteen years of guilt.

My hand trembles as I fit the key into the lock.

The door creaks open, and I step into the dimly lit foyer. The smell hits me first—a musty mix of old books and furniture polish that instantly transports me back to childhood summers. I close my eyes for a moment, half-expecting to hear Grandma Ingrid's voice calling me for dinner.

But when I open them, I'm alone in a silent house.

I drag my suitcase inside and flick on the light switch. The chandelier flickers to life, casting shadows across the faded wallpaper. Everything looks smaller than I remember, as if the house has shrunk in my absence.

My fingers trail along the banister as I climb the stairs, each step groaning under my weight. Family photos line the wall—familiar faces frozen in time. There's Mom and Dad on their wedding day, me gap-toothed and grinning at my fifth birthday party, Grandma Ingrid standing proud in her garden. I pause at a photo I don't recognize—a stern-looking man in an old-fashioned suit. His eyes seem to follow me as I continue up the stairs.

The second-floor hallway stretches before me, a row of closed doors hiding rooms I once knew by heart. I push open the first one—my old bedroom. The twin bed is still there, covered in a faded quilt. Dusty stuffed animals line the windowsill, their glass eyes reflecting the fading daylight.

A chill runs down my spine, and I rub my arms. It's colder in here than the rest of the house, despite the afternoon warmth outside. I shake off the feeling and move to the next room.

Grandma's bedroom is untouched, as if she might walk in at any moment. Her reading glasses sit on the nightstand next to a dog-eared mystery novel. The closet door stands slightly ajar, and I catch a whiff of her lavender perfume.

As I turn to leave, movement in the mirror catches my eye. I whirl around, heart pounding, but the room is empty. Just my imagination playing tricks on me.

I continue my exploration, each room stirring up memories—some warm, others bittersweet. But that nagging sense of unease follows me. The temperature seems to fluctuate from room to room, and more than once I catch myself glancing over my shoulder, unable to shake the feeling of being watched.

In the study, I pause to examine the old grandfather clock. Its steady ticking is the only sound in the quiet house. As I lean in to study the intricate carvings on its face, a floorboard creaks behind me.

I spin around, pulse racing. "Hello?" My voice echoes in the empty room. "Is someone there?"

I poke my head out into the hallway, heart still racing. "Hello?" I call again, my voice echoing off the walls. The house remains silent, save for the persistent ticking of the grandfather clock.

Suddenly, a familiar voice drifts up from downstairs. "Lena? You up there?"

Relief washes over me as I recognize Charlie's voice. I hurry down the stairs, my footsteps echoing in the empty house.

"Charlie? What are you doing here?"

She stands in the foyer, looking a bit sheepish. "I was thinking after we talked, and it just felt wrong leaving you alone to deal with... all of this." She gestures vaguely at the house around us.

I feel a rush of gratitude, touched by her thoughtfulness. "That's really sweet of you, Charlie. But I promise, I'll be okay."

She nods, but I can see the concern in her eyes. "Well, at least take my number. In case you need anything, or just want to talk."

"Thanks," I say, pulling out my phone. As I add her contact, a thought occurs to me. "Hey, where are you working these days?"

Charlie's face brightens. "Oh, I'm over at Hansen's Bakery on Main. One of the few places that hasn't changed much since we were kids."

I smile, remembering the sweet smell of cinnamon rolls that used to waft down the street. "I'm glad some things are still the same. I'll have to stop by for a bear claw—if Marie still makes them?"

"Every morning," Charlie laughs. "Some traditions are sacred in New Oslo."

We chat for a few more minutes, the familiar rhythm of our childhood friendship slowly returning. As Charlie turns to leave, I feel a little less alone in this big, empty house.

After Charlie leaves, I spend the rest of the afternoon sorting through Grandma's belongings, a bittersweet task that leaves me emotionally drained. As night falls, I heat up a can of soup I found in the pantry and settle in front of the TV, trying to ignore the oppressive silence of the house.

But as the clock ticks past midnight, the familiar creaks and groans of the old Victorian take on a more sinister tone. Every pop of settling wood makes me jump, and the shadows in the corners seem to stretch and dance in the flickering light of the TV.

Exhausted, I decide it's time for bed. I climb the stairs, wincing at each loud creak. In Grandma's room, I stare at her bed, neatly made with its floral comforter. The thought of sleeping there, surrounded by her things, makes my skin crawl. It feels wrong, like I'm intruding on her space.

I retreat to my childhood bedroom, but the twin bed proves to be a challenge. My feet hang off the end, and the mattress groans alarmingly when I try to get comfortable. After tossing and turning for what feels like hours, I give up.

Grabbing a blanket, I head back downstairs to the living room. The antique sofa isn't much better, its horsehair stuffing poking through in places, but at least I can stretch out. I curl up, trying to find a position that doesn't leave me with a spring digging into my side.

The house seems to come alive at night. The wind whistles through a gap in the window frame, creating an eerie howl. The pipes gurgle and clank, startling me just as I'm about to drift off. I pull the blanket tighter, feeling like a child afraid of the dark.

As I roll over for the hundredth time, movement catches my eye. I freeze, heart pounding. There, at the parlor window—a face, pale and indistinct, peering in at me. I blink, and it's gone, leaving me to wonder if it was ever there at all or just a trick of the moonlight on the old, warped glass.

Sleep eludes me as I lie there, eyes fixed on the window, straining to hear any sound of an intruder. But there's nothing except the usual noises of the house, which now seem to mock me with their persistence.

Chapter 2

I jolt awake, my heart pounding in my chest. A loud crash echoes through the house, too real to be a figment of my imagination. Sitting upright on the sofa, I blink rapidly, trying to adjust to the darkness. The old grandfather clock in the corner chimes once, signaling it's the middle of the night.

My hand fumbles along the coffee table, searching for something, anything I can use as a weapon. My fingers close around the cold, heavy brass of Grandma's favorite candlestick. I grip it tightly, its weight oddly comforting as I push myself to my feet.

Cautiously, I make my way through the living room, flicking on lights as I go. The sudden brightness makes me squint, but I force my eyes to stay open, scanning each room for any sign of an intruder.

The parlor is empty, save for the looming shadows cast by Grandma's antique furniture and a strange, perfumed scent I can't quite place. I move on to the dining room, my bare feet silent on the hardwood floor. Nothing seems out of place here either, but the crash definitely came from further in the house.

As I approach the kitchen, my grip on the candlestick tightens. My other hand hovers over the light switch, and I take a deep breath before flipping it on.

The fluorescent lights flicker to life, illuminating a scene that makes me gasp in shock. The candlestick slips from my fingers, clattering to the floor and narrowly missing my toes. But I barely notice, because standing at the counter, looking as real as the day I last saw her, is my grandmother.

She turns to face me, her familiar features etched with sadness. Her eyes, the same shade of blue as mine, meet my gaze, and I feel my knees go weak.

"Grandma?" I whisper, my voice barely audible over the pounding of my heart.

I take a hesitant step forward, my eyes locked on the familiar figure before me. As I draw closer, subtle differences in my grandmother's appearance begin to emerge. There's a faint shimmer around her edges, an almost ethereal quality that shouldn't be there. I squint, trying to focus, and realize with a jolt that I can see the outline of the cabinet doors through her body.

My breath catches in my throat. "This can't be real," I mutter, more to myself than to her.

Grandma's lips curve into a rueful smile. "I'm afraid it is, dear. Yes, I'm a ghost, and no, you're not hallucinating or having a nervous breakdown."

I blink rapidly, trying to process her words. "But... how?"

She chuckles softly, the sound achingly familiar. "Believe me, it was quite startling for me too. Woke up this way the day after it happened, in fact. Nearly scared poor Mr. Whiskers half to death when I tried to feed him. He lives next door with Harold now. Probably for the best."

I can't help but let out a strangled laugh at the thought of our old tomcat encountering a ghostly Grandma. It's so absurd, so impossible, and yet...

"Why are you here?" I ask, my voice barely above a whisper.

Grandma's expression turns serious. "I honestly don't know, but I have this feeling it has something to do with you, dear."

Right on cue, my nose starts to twitch. Almost like I need to sneeze, like I've just inhaled a whiff of dust or black pepper.

But no. It isn't a sneeze. It's the tell-tale sign that something isn't right.

My nose twitches again, more forcefully this time. I rub it with the back of my hand, trying to make it stop, but it's no use. Grandma's eyes widen, a spark of recognition lighting up her ghostly features.

"Oh my," she exclaims, floating closer. "Your nose! It's doing that thing again, isn't it?"

I nod, unable to speak as another twitch ripples across my face. Grandma reaches out as if to touch me, then seems to think better of it, her hand hovering just inches from my cheek.

"I should have known," she murmurs. "This is why I'm here. Your gift, it's acting up again."

"Gift?" I manage to sputter between twitches. "You mean this curse?"

Grandma tuts, shaking her head. "Now, now, Lena. We've talked about this. It's not a curse, it's a blessing. How many times has it saved you from real trouble?"

I sigh, knowing she's right. For as long as I can remember, my nose has had this uncanny ability to sense danger. It started when I was just a kid, a persistent twitch right before my best friend fell out of a tree and broke her arm. At first, everyone thought it was just a coincidence, a nervous tic.

But then it happened again. And again. A twitch before a car accident on our street. Another before a kitchen fire at school. Each time, my nose would start acting up, and soon after, something bad would happen.

"I know, I know," I concede. "But Grandma, it's never been this strong before. And you've never... well, you've never come back from the dead to warn me about it."

She chuckles, the sound both familiar and eerily distant. "Well, I suppose that means whatever's coming must be pretty serious, doesn't it?"

I feel a chill run down my spine at her words. "What do you think it could be?"

Grandma's expression turns thoughtful. "I'm not sure, dear. But I think we're about to find out. Your nose has never led us astray before."

As if on cue, another powerful twitch seizes my face, stronger than any I've felt before. I stumble back, catching myself on the kitchen counter. Grandma hovers nearby, her ghostly form flickering with concern.

Suddenly, a loud crash shatters the tense silence. The sound of breaking glass echoes through the house, making me jump.

"What was that?" I gasp, my heart racing.

Grandma's eyes widen. "I think it came from the parlor, dear."

Without thinking, I bolt from the kitchen, my bare feet slapping against the hardwood floor. Grandma glides alongside me, her ethereal form passing effortlessly through furniture and walls.

We burst into the parlor, and I skid to a halt, my breath catching in my throat. The scene before me sends a chill down my spine.

The large bay window, the one I could've sworn I saw someone standing outside of earlier, is now a gaping hole. Shards of glass litter the floor, glinting in the moonlight that streams through the broken pane. The wind howls through the opening, whipping the curtains into a frenzy.

"Oh my," Grandma whispers, her voice barely audible over the wind.

I take a cautious step forward, my eyes scanning the room. That's when I spot it—a large rock nestled among the glass shards, the obvious culprit behind the destruction.

"Grandma," I say, my voice shaking, "I think someone threw that rock through the window."

She nods gravely. "I believe you're right, Lena. And I have a feeling this is just the beginning of whatever your nose was warning us about."

I rub my nose, which has finally stopped twitching, and stare at the broken window. The memory of the shadowy figure I thought I saw earlier flashes through my mind, and a chill runs down my spine.

"What do we do now?" I ask, turning to face my ghostly grandmother.

Grandma's ethereal form flickers as she considers my question. Her brow furrows, a habit I remember so well from when she was alive.

"We can't do much tonight, dear," she says, her voice tinged with concern. "It's too dark, too dangerous to go poking around outside now. You should call the police, but leave the investigating up to them."

I nod, reluctantly agreeing. The idea of waiting around in here like a sitting duck feels wrong, but I know she's right. We'd be at a disadvantage stumbling around in the dark. Besides, I'll feel a lot better once the police get here to check things out.

"But Grandma," I start, a thought suddenly occurring to me, "why are you here? I mean, why now?"

She sighs, a sound that seems to echo through the room despite her incorporeal state. "I've been thinking about that, Lena. And I can't shake the feeling that my death is somehow connected to all this."

My eyes widen. "What do you mean?"

"That crackpot coroner said I died of natural causes," she scoffs, shaking her head. "But I know better. There was someone behind my death, I'm sure of it."

A chill runs down my spine at her words. "Someone... murdered you?"

Grandma nods solemnly. "I can't prove it, but I feel it in my bones... well, if I still had any." She attempts a weak smile at her own joke.

"But why?" I ask, my mind reeling. "Who would want to hurt you?"

"I don't know, dear," she admits. "But I have a terrible feeling they might not be done. I just hope..." she trails off, her ghostly eyes filled with worry.

"Hope what?"

"I hope they haven't come back to make sure you meet the same fate."

The words hang heavy in the air between us. I feel my heart racing, the implications of what she's saying sinking in. Someone might have killed my grandmother, and now they could be after me.

Chapter 3

I wake up with a start, my heart pounding as the events of last night come rushing back. The broken window, the rock, and most importantly, my grandmother's ghost. It all feels like a bizarre dream, but the shards of glass still littering the parlor floor are a stark reminder of reality.

I need to talk to someone, someone who won't think I'm completely insane. Charlie. She's always been there for me, and right now, I desperately need a friendly face.

Without bothering to change out of my rumpled clothes from yesterday, I grab my keys and dash out the door. The morning air is crisp as I make my way to the bakery where Charlie works. Everything about this situation is crazy, but what else am I supposed to do?

I burst in, startling a few early morning customers. Charlie looks up from behind the counter, her usual cheerful smile faltering as she takes in my disheveled appearance.

"Lena? What's wrong?" she quickly hands off a paper bag to a customer before making her way around the counter.

"I need to talk to you," I say, my voice shaky. "It's... it's about Grandma."

Charlie's brow furrows with concern. She glances at the clock, then nods. "Give me five minutes to hand things over to Sarah. We can talk in the back."

I nod gratefully, pacing near the door while Charlie speaks quietly with her coworker. My mind races, trying to figure out how to explain what happened without sounding completely unhinged.

Finally, she leads me to the small office in the back of the bakery. The smell of sugar and warm dough is comforting, grounding me as I try to collect my thoughts.

"Okay, Lena," she says, closing the door behind us. "What's going on?"

I take a deep breath, then let it all spill out. The twitching nose, the broken window, and most importantly, my grandmother's ghost. Charlie listens intently, her expression a mix of concern and disbelief.

"I know how it sounds," I say, wringing my hands. "I'm not even sure if I believe it myself. Am I going crazy, Charlie? Or did my dead grandmother really talk to me last night?"

Charlie runs a hand through her hair, flour dust puffing into the air. "That's... a lot to take in, Lena. Did you call the police? About the broken window, I mean?"

I nod, feeling a mix of frustration and embarrassment. "Yeah, I called the sheriff's office last night. A deputy came out, but he was... less than helpful."

Charlie leans against the desk, her brow furrowed. "What do you mean?"

I sigh, recalling the deputy's dismissive attitude. "He barely looked around. Just glanced at the broken window, asked if anything was stolen, and then acted like I was wasting his time."

"That's ridiculous," Charlie says, crossing her arms. "Did you tell him about... you know, your grandmother?"

I let out a bitter laugh. "God, no. He already thought I was overreacting about the window. If I'd mentioned seeing a ghost, he probably would've hauled me off to the psych ward."

Charlie nods sympathetically. "So what did he say about the rock?"

"He said it was probably just some kids causing trouble. Told me to sweep up the glass and get the window fixed. That was pretty much it."

I start pacing the small office, my frustration building. "I mean, I get it. Small town, not much crime. But you'd think a broken window would at least warrant a proper investigation."

"Did he file a report?" Charlie asks.

I shake my head. "He said there wasn't much point without any leads or stolen property. Told me to call back if anything else happened."

Charlie's expression darkens. "That's not right, Lena. You should file a complaint."

"And say what? That I'm upset because the deputy didn't believe my ghost story?" I run a hand through my hair, feeling overwhelmed. "I don't even know if I believe it myself."

Charlie steps forward, placing a comforting hand on my arm. "Look, ghost or no ghost, something happened last night. You deserve to be taken seriously."

I nod, grateful for her support. "Thanks, Charlie. I just... I don't know what to do next. I can't shake the feeling that there's more going on here than just some random vandalism."

Charlie's eyes light up with determination. "You know what? Let's go to the police station right now. I'll come with you to talk to Sheriff Mark."

I blink, surprised by her sudden enthusiasm. "Sheriff Mark? Do I know him?"

"Probably! He was a few years ahead of us in school. And his family owns the bakery—his mom's my boss," she explains, already reaching for her coat. "He's a good guy, I think he'll listen if we both go."

The idea of confronting the sheriff makes my stomach churn, but Charlie's confidence is contagious. "Okay," I nod, taking a deep breath. "Let's do it."

We make our way to the police station, a small brick building that looks more like a quaint house than a center of law enforcement.

Sheriff Mark glances up from his desk, recognition flickering across his face. "Charlie, right? And... Lena?" He stands, offering a polite smile. "What can I do for you ladies?"

Charlie takes charge, her voice steady and surprisingly authoritative. "We're here about the incident at Lena's house last night. The broken window?"

Mark's brow furrows slightly. "Ah, yes. I believe Deputy Mickelson responded to that call."

"He did," I say, finding my voice. "But I don't think he took it seriously enough."

Mark leans back against his desk, arms crossed. "Oh? What makes you say that?"

I take a deep breath, steeling myself. "Someone threw a rock through my window, Sheriff. That's not just kids causing trouble. I think... I think someone might be targeting me."

Mark's expression remains neutral, but I catch a flicker of skepticism in his eyes. "That's a pretty serious accusation, Lena. I keep pretty close tabs on what goes on here in town, and I didn't even know you were back. Do you have any evidence to support your suspicion?"

I hesitate, glancing at Charlie. How can I explain about my grandmother's ghost without sounding completely unhinged?

Charlie steps in, her voice firm. "Evidence or not, Sheriff, a crime was committed. Doesn't that warrant a proper investigation?"

Mark holds up his hands in a placating gesture. "Now, I'm not saying we won't look into it. But without any leads or witnesses, there's only so much we can do."

I feel my frustration rising. "So, what? I'm just supposed to wait until they decide to break another window? Or worse?"

Mark's expression softens, and he leans forward, his voice taking on a gentler tone. "Look, Lena, I understand you're upset. It's not easy coming back to an empty house full of memories. Especially your grandmother's place—she was quite a character."

I feel a surge of frustration. "This isn't about grief, Mark. Someone broke my window! They could've very easily entered the house while I was right there sleeping."

He holds up a hand. "I hear you. But the fact of the matter is that nobody broke in, did they? Yes, the window was broken. I understand and sympathize. It could have very well been a crime, but it could have also been an accident. It could've been the wind, for all we know. There isn't always a threat lurking around every corner."

Charlie steps closer, her voice tight. "Are you saying you don't believe her?"

Mark sighs, running a hand through his hair. "That's not what I'm saying at all. I'm just suggesting that maybe this situation isn't as dire as it seems. Lena, you've been through a lot. Spending the night alone in that big old house, it's bound to stir up some emotions."

I clench my fists, trying to keep my voice steady. "So you're not going to do anything?"

"Now, I didn't say that," Mark says, reaching for his phone. "Tell you what, I'll call over to Miller's Hardware right now. We'll get that window replaced today, my treat. It's the least I can do for an old friend who's had a less-than-warm welcome back home."

Old friend? I've never been so tempted to smack a police officer—or anyone else, for that matter—so hard before.

I open my mouth to argue, but Charlie puts a hand on my arm, giving a slight shake of her head.

Mark dials, his voice cheery as he speaks to someone on the other end. "Hey, Tom! It's Sheriff Mark. Listen, I've got a bit of an emergency job for you. Lena Larsen is back in town, staying at her grandmother's old place. Seems a rock or branch or something came down and broke one of the windows. Think you could head over there today and get it fixed up?"

He pauses, listening, then nods. "Great, thanks Tom. I appreciate it." He hangs up and turns back to us with a smile. "There you go. Tom will be over in about an hour to take care of that window. Is there anything else I can do for you ladies?"

I feel deflated, all the fight draining out of me. "No, I guess that's it. Thanks."

Mark nods, his expression sympathetic. "Take care, Lena. And don't hesitate to call if you need anything else. You know we look out for our own around here."

As Charlie and I turn to leave, I can't shake the feeling that I've just been patted on the head and sent on my way. The broken window will be fixed, but the real problem—whatever it is—remains unaddressed.

Chapter 4

I storm out of the sheriff's office, Charlie close on my heels. The crisp morning air does little to cool my temper.

"Can you believe that?" I fume, pacing on the sidewalk. "He basically called me hysterical!"

Charlie's face is a mask of concern. "I'm sorry, Lena. That was... not great."

I take a deep breath, trying to calm myself. "You know what? Forget him. If the sheriff won't take this seriously, I'll figure it out myself."

Charlie raises an eyebrow. "What do you mean?"

"I mean, I'm going to investigate. Starting with Grandma's house. There has to be something there, some clue about what really happened to her."

Charlie hesitates. "Are you sure that's a good idea?"

I nod, determination setting in. "I have to do something. Are you with me?"

She sighs but nods. "Of course. Let's go."

We drive back to the house in silence. As we pull up, I see Tom from the hardware store already there, measuring the broken window. I wave to him as we pass, heading straight for the front door.

Inside, I stand in the entryway, surveying the familiar space with new eyes. "Okay, where do we start?"

Charlie shrugs. "If I were hiding something important, I'd probably keep it in my bedroom."

"Good thinking," I say, heading for the stairs. "Let's start there."

In Grandma Ingrid's room, everything looks untouched. I run my hand over her old vanity, remembering how she used to brush my hair here when I was little.

"What exactly are we looking for?" Charlie asks, opening a drawer.

"I'm not sure," I admit. "Anything suspicious. Anything that might explain why she died so suddenly."

We search methodically, careful not to disturb things too much. I check under the mattress, in the closet, behind picture frames. Nothing seems out of place.

I'm rifling through Grandma's dresser when my fingers brush against something that doesn't feel like fabric. Frowning, I pull out a stack of envelopes, yellowed with age.

"Charlie, look at this," I call out, my heart racing.

She hurries over as I open the first envelope with trembling hands. Inside is a single sheet of paper, the message composed of cut-out letters from magazines:

"LEAVE NOW OR FACE THE CONSEQUENCES."

My blood runs cold. "What in the world?"

Charlie peers over my shoulder, her face pale. "When is that from?"

I check the postmark on the envelope. "Three months ago."

We exchange worried glances before I tear into the next one. The message is similar, but more specific:

"THE HOUSE ISN'T YOURS. GET OUT WHILE YOU STILL CAN."

My hands shake as I open envelope after envelope. Each note becomes more threatening, more urgent. The final one, dated just a week before Grandma's death, chills me to the bone:

"LAST WARNING. LEAVE OR DIE."

I sink onto the bed, my mind reeling. "Charlie, these... these are death threats. Someone was trying to force Grandma out of her home."

Charlie's eyes are wide with shock. "But why? And who would do such a thing?"

I shake my head, trying to process this new information. "I don't know, but it can't be a coincidence that she died right after receiving these."

I clutch the threatening letters in my hands, my mind racing. That's when I catch it—a faint, slightly familiar scent wafting through the air. My nose twitches as I try to place it.

"Do you smell that?" I ask Charlie, frowning.

She sniffs the air, looking confused. "Smell what?"

"It's... I can't quite place it, but I've smelled it before." Then it hits me. "Last night. When the window broke downstairs. It's the same scent."

Charlie's eyes widen. "Are you sure?"

I nod, getting to my feet. "Positive. It's faint, but it's definitely the same smell. We need to keep looking."

We continue our search with renewed vigor, pulling out drawers and checking behind every picture frame. The scent seems to grow stronger as we move towards Grandma's closet.

"Wait," Charlie says, pointing to a small wooden chest tucked away in the corner. "Have you checked that?"

I shake my head and kneel down, running my hands over the intricate carvings on the lid. It's locked, but the key is hanging on a thin chain around the latch. With trembling fingers, I unlock it and lift the lid.

Inside, nestled among old photographs and trinkets, is a leather-bound book. My heart skips a beat as I recognize my grandmother's handwriting on the cover: "Ingrid's Journal."

"Charlie," I breathe, "I think we've found something."

I carefully lift the journal out of the chest, the leather cool and smooth against my palms.

I open the journal with shaking hands, the musty scent of old paper filling my nostrils. Charlie leans in close as we begin to read.

The first few entries are mundane, detailing Grandma's daily life—her garden, her knitting projects, visits from neighbors. But as I flip through the pages, the tone shifts dramatically.

"May 15th: I can't shake the feeling that someone's watching me. When I'm in the garden, I swear I see movement in the woods. But every time I look, there's nothing there. Am I going crazy?"

My heart races as I turn to the next entry.

"May 20th: The letters keep coming. I don't know what they want from me, but I'm scared. I've lived in this house for fifty years. It's all I have left of Harold. I can't leave, I won't."

Charlie's grip on my arm tightens as we read on.

"June 2nd: I heard noises downstairs last night. When I went to check, nothing was out of place, but that smell... it was there again. What's happening to me?"

I swallow hard, remembering the scent from last night and just moments ago. Is it the same one Grandma described?

"June 10th: I'm afraid to sleep. Every creak, every shadow makes me jump. I should call Lena, but I don't want to worry her. Maybe if I ignore it, it'll go away."

Tears prick my eyes as I read the growing desperation in Grandma's words. Why didn't she call me?

"June 15th: The threats are getting worse. I found a dead bird on my porch this morning. Its neck was broken. This isn't just pranks anymore. Someone really wants me gone. But where would I go? This is my home."

The entries grow shorter, more frantic. Grandma writes about feeling constantly on edge, about strange symbols appearing on her property, about whispers in the night that she can't quite make out.

The final entry, dated just two days before her death, makes my blood run cold:

"I can't take this anymore. They're closing in. I don't know who to trust. If anything happens to me, Lena, know that I lo-"

The sentence cuts off abruptly, a long ink line trailing off the page as if Grandma had been interrupted mid-writing.

I close the journal, my hands trembling. "Charlie," I whisper, my voice thick with emotion, "Grandma didn't just die. She was murdered."

"Lena?" Charlie's voice breaks through my shock. "Are you okay?"

I look up at her, tears blurring my vision. "How could this happen? Why didn't she tell me?"

Charlie wraps an arm around my shoulders. "She probably didn't want to worry you. But Lena, this changes everything."

I nod, wiping my eyes. "You're right. The sheriff needs to see this. He can't ignore evidence like this."

"And if he does?" Charlie asks, her tone careful.

I stand up, clutching the journal to my chest. "Then we'll find someone who will listen. The state police, the FBI, whoever it takes. I'm not letting this go, Charlie. Someone murdered my grandmother, and they're going to pay for it."

Charlie nods, her eyes filled with determination. "We'll figure this out, Lena. Together. Where do you want to start?"

I take a deep breath, my mind racing. "We need to go through everything in this house. There might be more clues, more evidence. And we should talk to the neighbors, see if they noticed anything suspicious."

"Good idea," Charlie says. "And what about that smell you mentioned? Maybe we can figure out what it is, trace it somehow."

I nod, feeling a spark of hope. "Yes, definitely. And we should look into who might have wanted Grandma's property. These threats, they kept mentioning the house. There has to be a reason."

As we talk, I feel my shock and grief transforming into something else—a fierce determination to uncover the truth. Grandma deserved better than this, and I'm going to make sure she gets justice.

"We're not letting this go," I say, my voice stronger now. "No matter what it takes, we're going to find out who did this to Grandma."

Charlie squeezes my hand. "I'm with you all the way, Lena. We'll solve this, I promise."

Chapter 5

I sit on the worn sofa in Grandma's living room, now my living room, surrounded by stacks of papers and old photographs. The weight of the unsolved mystery presses down on me, making it hard to breathe. How am I ever going to figure this out?

Charlie left an hour ago, promising to return tomorrow with fresh eyes and new ideas. But right now, in the quiet of the house, I feel utterly lost.

"Oh, Grandma," I whisper, "I wish you could tell me what happened."

My nose twitches—something I've been noticing more and more lately—and the air around me shifts. I look up, and there she is – Grandma's ghost, shimmering in the fading evening light.

"Lena, dear," she says, her voice echoing softly. "You look troubled."

I laugh, a short, bitter sound. "Troubled doesn't begin to cover it, Grandma. I found your journal. I know someone was threatening you, that you were murdered. But I don't know how to prove it or who did it. The sheriff won't listen, and I'm running out of ideas. Do you... do you remember anything that might help?"

Grandma's form flickers, her brow furrowing. "I'm afraid my memories of that time are hazy, dear. Being a ghost isn't all it's cracked up to be." She chuckles, but it's a hollow sound. "But you know, there is something that's been nagging at me."

I lean forward, hope blooming in my chest. "What is it?"

"Well, it's probably nothing, but... it's awfully interesting how quickly old Harold made it over to the house when I died. He was one of the first people on the scene."

"Harold? Your neighbor?" I ask, surprised. "But he's always been so kind."

Grandma nods, her form wavering. "Oh, he has. But you know what they say—it's always the ones you least expect."

Harold? Sweet old Harold who always brought over fresh-baked cookies? It seems impossible, but...

"You're right, Grandma. I can't rule anyone out." I stand up, pacing the room. "I'll go talk to him tomorrow morning. Maybe he saw something. Or maybe he knows something he didn't realize was important at the time."

Or maybe, like Grandma suggests, he's a suspect himself.

Grandma's ghost nods, a proud smile on her face. "That's my girl. Now get some rest, dear. You look exhausted."

As her form fades away, I realize just how tired I am. I trudge up to bed, my mind racing with questions about Harold. Sleep comes in fits and starts, filled with dreams of shadowy figures and whispered threats.

When the first rays of sunlight peek through my curtains, I'm already wide awake. I throw on some clothes and gulp down a cup of coffee, determined to get answers.

The walk next door to Harold's house is only a few yards, but feels longer than it should. Each step sends my heart racing a little faster. What if Grandma's right? What if Harold isn't who I thought he was?

I reach his front porch and take a deep breath. Here goes nothing. I raise my hand and knock on the door.

"Harold? It's Lena. From next door." My voice sounds steady, but my heart is pounding in my ears. I hear shuffling from inside, and the door swings open. Harold stands there, his eyes widening at the sight of me.

"Lena, my dear," he says, his voice cracking. "What brings you here so early?"

I square my shoulders. "I need to talk to you about Grandma Ingrid. About what happened to her."

Harold's gaze shifts to the side, and he bites his lip. "Of course, of course. Come in, come in." He ushers me inside, his nervousness palpable. "Can I get you some tea?"

"No, thank you." I stay standing, my eyes scanning the room. "I've been going through Grandma's things, and I found her journal. She wrote about feeling threatened before she died. I'm trying to figure out what happened, who might've wanted to hurt her."

Harold's eyes flick back to me, his face paling. "Threatened? Oh dear. I had no idea."

His reaction catches my attention – he looks genuinely surprised, but is it an act? "You were close to Grandma. Closer than most, I think." I watch him carefully, gauging his response.

Harold fidgets with his sleeve. "Well, yes. We were neighbors for many years. Good friends."

"So, you must've noticed if she was acting strange before she died. Any unusual visitors? Anything out of the ordinary?" I press, my voice sharp.

"I..." Harold stammers, his eyes darting around the room. "I can't say I did, no. We didn't see each other as much toward the end. She was keeping to herself more."

"But you were one of the first people to find her after she died," I persist, stepping forward. "You must've seen or heard something. The police said it looked like a break-in gone wrong."

"I... I was just passing by and saw the broken window." Harold backs away, his voice shaking. "I didn't see or hear anything useful, I'm afraid. The poor woman."

I watch Harold carefully, my eyes narrowing as he stammers through his explanation. Something doesn't feel right. As he speaks, my nose twitches—that strange sensation I've been experiencing more frequently since Grandma's death. It's like an itch I can't scratch, a warning signal flaring in my mind.

"Harold," I say, cutting him off mid-sentence. "Are you sure there's nothing else you can tell me? Anything at all?"

He wrings his hands, avoiding my gaze. "I'm sorry, Lena. I wish I could be of more help."

My nose twitches again, more insistently this time. It's as if my body is trying to tell me something my conscious mind hasn't quite grasped yet. I can't shake the feeling that Harold is hiding something, but what?

I take a step closer, studying his face. Beads of sweat have formed on his forehead, and his eyes keep darting to the side, never quite meeting mine. Is it just the discomfort of discussing Grandma's death, or is there more to it?

"You know," I say, keeping my voice casual, "Grandma always spoke so highly of you. She said you were one of the few people she could truly trust."

Harold's face contorts, a mix of guilt and something else—fear?—flashing across his features. "Ingrid was... she was a dear friend," he mumbles.

My nose twitches again, more violently this time. I fight the urge to rub it, instead focusing all my attention on Harold. He's definitely hiding something, but I can't put my finger on what it might be. Is he protecting someone? Or is he more directly involved than I initially thought?

I decide to push a little harder. "Harold, if there's anything you're not telling me, now's the time. I'm not going to stop until I figure out what happened to Grandma. If you know something—anything—please, help me understand."

Harold's shoulders slump, and for a moment, I think he's going to confess. But then he straightens up, a forced smile on his face. "I'm sorry, Lena. I truly don't know anything more. Now, if you'll excuse me, I have some errands to run."

As he ushers me towards the door, my nose twitches one last time. I'm certain now that Harold is keeping secrets, but I'm no closer to understanding what they might be. I step out onto the porch, my mind racing with new questions and theories.

Chapter 6

I pull out my phone and dial Charlie's number, hoping she can help me locate Annika. After a few rings, she picks up.

"Hey, Lena. What's up?"

"Charlie, I need a favor. I need to get in touch with my cousin Annika, and I haven't talked to her in years. Grandma said she's apparently back in town as of a few months ago. Do you happen to know where she lives?"

There's a pause on the other end. "Annika? Your cousin? Yeah, I think I do. Why do you need to know?"

I hesitate, not wanting to worry her in case it turns out to be another dead end. "It's related to Grandma's death. Or... her will, I guess. I just need to talk to her in person."

Charlie's voice turns serious. "Okay, let me check my contacts. I think I have her address from when we sent out invitations for our class reunion a few years back."

I wait impatiently as I hear her shuffling through papers. Finally, she comes back on the line.

"Got it. You ready?"

I grab a pen and scribble down the address as she reads it out. "Thanks, Charlie. I owe you one."

"No problem. Just... be careful, okay? And let me know if you need anything else."

I hang up and stare at the address for a moment before grabbing my keys and heading out the door. The drive across town takes about fifteen minutes, just enough time to wonder what I'm going to say to Annika when I see her.

As I turn onto her street, I scan the house numbers until I spot the one I'm looking for. Annika's place is smaller than I expected, an older house with faded blue siding and a small front porch. Despite its age, it looks well-maintained, with neatly trimmed bushes lining the walkway.

I park my car and steel myself for whatever might come next. As I walk up to the front door, I notice a wind chime hanging from the porch roof, tinkling softly in the breeze. It's a peaceful sound, at odds with the tension I feel coiling in my stomach.

Standing on the porch, I raise my hand to knock, wondering how Annika will react to my unexpected visit. Will she be surprised? Suspicious? Or maybe she's been expecting someone to come asking questions. Only one way to find out.

I knock on the door, my heart pounding. After a moment, I hear footsteps approaching. The door swings open, and there stands Annika, her eyes widening in surprise.

"Lena?" she gasps, her hand still on the doorknob. "What are you doing here?"

I take in her appearance—she looks older than I remember, her once-vibrant red hair now streaked with a few strands of gray. But her green eyes, so like Grandma's, are as sharp as ever.

"Hi, Annika," I say, trying to keep my voice steady. "It's been a while."

She nods, her expression shifting from shock to wariness. "Yes, it has. How did you find me?"

"I asked around," I reply vaguely. "Listen, I need to talk to you about something important. Can I come in?"

Annika hesitates, glancing over her shoulder into the house. "I'm not sure that's a good idea. I'm kind of in the middle of something."

I can see her starting to close off, and I know I need to act fast. "It's about our inheritance," I blurt out. "From Grandma."

Her hand tightens on the doorknob, and I see a flicker of something—interest? Concern?—in her eyes. She looks at me for a long moment, as if weighing her options.

Finally, she sighs and steps back. "Fine, come in. But I don't have much time."

I follow her into a small, cluttered living room. Books and papers are scattered across every surface, and the air smells faintly of something familiar that I can't quite place. Incense? Perfume? Whatever it is, it's tugging at the edges of my mind as Annika clears a stack of newspapers off the couch and gestures for me to sit.

"So," she says, perching on the edge of an armchair across from me. "What's this about an inheritance?"

I take a deep breath, trying to figure out how to approach this without revealing too much. "Well, it's... complicated," I start, fidgeting with the hem of my shirt. "I'm still going through all the paperwork, you know how it is with legal stuff."

Annika's eyes narrow slightly. "Uh-huh. And you came all the way here just to tell me that?"

"Not exactly," I say, thinking fast. "I was hoping you might have some information that could help. Did Grandma ever mention anything to you about her will? Or maybe you saw a copy of it at some point?"

She leans back in her chair, crossing her arms. "Lena, I haven't spoken to Grandma in years. Why would she show me her will?"

I shrug, trying to appear nonchalant. "I don't know. I just thought maybe... since you were back in town..."

"That doesn't mean I was in contact with her," Annika interrupts, her tone sharp. "Look, if there's an inheritance, shouldn't the lawyer have all the details?"

I nod, feeling sweat prickle at the back of my neck. "Yeah, of course. It's just... there are some discrepancies we're trying to sort out. I thought maybe you might know something that could help clear things up."

Annika's expression softens slightly, but I can still see suspicion in her eyes. "I'm sorry, but I really don't know anything about Grandma's will or any inheritance. Is that all you came here for?"

I hesitate, knowing I need to keep her talking but unsure how to proceed. "Well, I was also hoping we could catch up a bit. It's been so long, and with Grandma gone..." I trail off, hoping to appeal to her sense of family.

She sighs, uncrossing her arms. "Lena, I appreciate the thought, but now's not really a good time. I've got a lot going on."

I glance around the cluttered room, noticing for the first time the strange symbols scrawled on some of the papers. "What kind of work do you do?" I ask, genuinely curious.

Annika's eyes dart around the room, avoiding my gaze. "Oh, you know, this and that. Freelance work mostly. Nothing too exciting."

I nod, trying to keep her engaged. "Sounds interesting. What kind of freelance work?"

She shifts in her seat, her fingers drumming on the armrest. "Writing, mostly. Look, Lena, I don't mean to be rude, but I really do have a lot to do today."

I can feel the conversation slipping away from me. "Right, of course. I just thought maybe we could catch up a bit more. It's been so long, and with everything that's happened..."

Annika stands abruptly, cutting me off. "I'm sorry, but I really can't right now. Maybe we can get coffee sometime next week?"

Her tone makes it clear that 'next week' might as well be 'never'. I nod, trying to hide my disappointment. "Sure, that sounds nice. I'll give you a call."

I slowly get to my feet, glancing around the room one last time. As Annika moves past me to lead the way to the door, something catches my eye. Among the scattered papers on the coffee table, I spot a colorful flyer for a real estate developer.

Without thinking, I reach out and snatch the flyer, quickly slipping it into my purse. My heart races as I follow Annika to the door, hoping she didn't notice.

"Thanks for stopping by," she says, her hand already on the doorknob. "Take care, Lena."

I step out onto the porch, feeling the weight of the flyer in my purse. "You too, Annika. I'll be in touch."

As the door closes behind me, I can't shake the feeling that I've just crossed a line. But something about that flyer seemed important, and I couldn't let the opportunity slip away.

Chapter 7

I drive home, my mind racing with thoughts about Annika's strange behavior and the flyer I swiped. As I turn onto my street, I notice an unfamiliar car parked in my driveway. It's sleek and expensive-looking, definitely out of place in this neighborhood.

Before I can even step out of my car, I see a shimmer in the air. Grandma's ghost materializes right in front of me as soon as my foot touches the property.

"Lena, dear," she says, her voice urgent. "That man in the car, I don't trust him."

I glance towards the vehicle, then back at Grandma. "Who is he? Do you know him?"

She frowns, her spectral form flickering slightly. "I can't remember exactly how I know him, but something's not right. Be careful, sweetie."

"Wait, Grandma—" I start, but she's already fading away. "Don't go! I have so many questions!"

But it's too late. She's gone, leaving me alone with more mysteries than answers. I hear a car door slam and footsteps approaching.

I turn to see a man walking toward me, his smile too wide, too bright, and obviously fake. He's dressed in an expensive suit that screams 'corporate,' and his hair is slicked back in a way that makes me think he's definitely going to try and sell me something.

"Ms. Lena Larsen?" he calls out, his hand already outstretched. "Victor Dahl. It's a pleasure to meet you."

As he gets closer, I recognize him from the flyer I took from Annika's house. He's the property developer, and suddenly, I have a sinking feeling about why he might be here.

I stand there, frozen, as he approaches. His smile never wavers, but there's something unsettling about it, like a shark circling its prey.

"Ms. Larsen, I was so sorry to hear about your grandmother's passing," he says, his voice dripping with false sympathy. "She was a remarkable woman."

I shake his hand briefly, then step back. "Thank you, Mr. Dahl. She certainly was. What can I do for you?"

His eyes gleam with barely concealed interest. "Well, I was wondering if the estate had been settled yet. I know these things can take time, but I couldn't help but be curious about your plans for the house."

A chill runs down my spine. "My plans?"

"Yes, yes. Are you the actual owner now? Or is it still in probate?" He leans in, his voice lowering conspiratorially. "Because if you're thinking of selling, I'd be more than happy to make you an offer. This property has... potential."

Before I can respond, the air around us shimmers. Grandma's ghost materializes, her translucent form practically vibrating with fury. Her eyes are fixed on Victor, and if looks could kill, he'd be six feet under.

"You!" she hisses, her voice echoing with otherworldly anger. "I remember you now, Victor Dahl!"

Of course, Victor can't hear or see her, but I can. And what I see are all the missing memories flooding back to my grandmother's spectral form.

"This snake," she spits, gesturing wildly at Victor, "He's been trying to get his hands on our home for years! Always showing up with his fancy suits and fake smiles, offering to 'take this old place off my hands.' As if I'd ever sell to the likes of him!"

I glance between Grandma's furious ghost and Victor's oblivious, grinning face. The contrast is jarring.

"He was relentless, Lena," Grandma continues, her voice trembling with rage. "Especially in the months before I died. Always 'dropping by' with new offers, talking about how I shouldn't burden my family with an old house. As if our home was nothing but a burden!"

I stand there, caught between Victor's eager sales pitch and Grandma's spectral fury. It's surreal, watching him gesture animatedly about property values while Grandma's ghost paces behind him, her transparent form practically crackling with indignation.

"You see, Ms. Larsen," Victor continues, oblivious to the supernatural drama unfolding around him, "this area is primed for development. Your grandmother's property could be the cornerstone of a whole new—"

"Don't you dare listen to him, Lena!" Grandma interjects, her voice echoing in my head. "He'll turn our home into a parking lot if you let him!"

I blink rapidly, trying to focus on Victor's words while Grandma's warnings ring in my ears. It's like trying to listen to two radio stations at once, and I'm sure my distraction is showing on my face.

Victor pauses mid-sentence, his brow furrowing. "Ms. Larsen? Are you feeling okay?"

"I'm fine," I manage, forcing a smile. "Please, go on."

He resumes his pitch, but I notice his eyes darting around, almost as if he can sense something's off. At one point, he stops abruptly, his gaze fixed on the exact spot where Grandma's ghost is standing. For a moment, I wonder if he can actually see her, but then he shakes his head and continues.

"As I was saying, the potential here is enormous. Now, I'd love to go over some options with you if you have the time." Victor's already moving toward the front porch, his body language confident, as if he's certain I'll invite him in.

Grandma's ghost moves to block his path, her arms spread wide. "Don't you dare let this snake into our home, Lena!"

I step forward quickly. "Mr. Dahl, I appreciate your interest, but now isn't a good time. I've got a splitting headache coming on, and I really need to lie down."

Victor's smile falters for a moment, his eyes narrowing. "Oh, I see. Well, perhaps we could schedule a time to talk later this week? I have some very exciting proposals that I'm sure you'll want to hear."

I shake my head, wincing for effect. "I'm sorry, but I'm going to need some time. This is all still very fresh, you understand. My grandmother's passing, inheriting the house... I need to process everything before I make any decisions."

The change in Victor's demeanor is subtle but noticeable. His smile becomes fixed, almost plastic, and his eyes lose their practiced, fake warmth. "Of course, of course. I completely understand. Grief is a process, after all."

He reaches into his jacket pocket and pulls out a business card that's attached to a folded brochure that matches the one in my purse. "Here's my card. When you're ready to discuss the future of this property, give me a call. I'll be waiting."

The way he says "waiting" sends a chill down my spine. It sounds less like patience and more like a threat.

"Thank you, Mr. Dahl. I'll be in touch when I'm ready," I say, taking the card and pocketing it without looking at it.

Victor nods curtly, his earlier charm completely evaporated. "See that you do, Ms. Larsen. Opportunities like this don't come along every day."

He turns on his heel and strides back to his car. I watch as he drives away, his tires squealing slightly as he accelerates down the street.

As soon as he's out of sight, I let out a long breath I didn't realize I was holding. Grandma's ghost reappears beside me, the pride and concern clear in her expression.

"Well done, Lena," she says softly. "But be careful. That man won't give up easily."

I nod, my mind racing with questions. "Grandma, we need to talk. There's so much I don't understand."

She smiles gently. "I know, dear. Let's go inside. We have a lot to discuss."

I follow Grandma into the house, my heart still pounding from the encounter with Victor. I half expect him to come barging in, but the door swings shut behind us, solid and reassuring.

"Sit, Lena," Grandma says, gesturing to one of the chairs at the kitchen table. I do, and she sits across from me, her form shimmering slightly but still solid enough to be unmistakably real.

"What about the deed, Grandma? Annika—she was acting so strange, like I was bothering her the entire tome—is she entitled to part of the house? Maybe I should sell it and split the money with her." My voice wavers as I struggle to process this sudden revelation about my family.

Grandma's expression softens. "Absolutely not, dear. The deed will be transferred to your name once you go to the courthouse and sign the paperwork. Your cousin has already received a few things from me, and that's all I intended for her to have."

I bite my lip. "But is that fair? She's family, after all."

"Blood doesn't always define family, Lena. I made my decision for a reason. If Annika wanted a relationship, she would have reached out long ago. Don't you go second-guessing my wishes now, you hear?"

I nod, feeling a weight lift from my shoulders. "Okay, Grandma. I trust you."

She pats my hand gently, and it's a warm, reassuring sensation even though I can't actually feel her touch. "I know, dear. Now, about the house... If it truly becomes a burden, you can sell it. But I'd like you to try and keep it in the family if you can. At least for a little while."

My eyes prick with tears at her understanding. "I promise I'll do everything I can to keep it, Grandma. This house holds so many memories. I'd love for my future children to run around the same yard I did, pick apples from the old tree."

Grandma's ghost smiles, her eyes glittering. "I'm glad to hear that, Lena. This old house has a lot of love left to give."

I take a deep breath, steeling myself for what I need to ask next. "Grandma, why can I see you? Why haven't you... moved on? And what's it like... wherever you are?"

Grandma's smile fades, replaced by a look of concentration. "That's a tough one to answer, dear. It's... not easy to describe."

I lean forward, eager to understand. "Please try, Grandma. I want to know."

She furrows her brow. "Well, when I'm not here with you, it's like... a fog. Dense and thick. I can't see or hear anything clearly. It's as if I'm asleep, but not quite."

"That sounds awful," I whisper.

Grandma shakes her head. "It's not painful or scary. Just... confusing. But then, when I sense you need me, the fog starts to thin. It becomes less dense, and I can make out shapes and sounds. Always some part of the house or the property."

I glance around the familiar kitchen. "So you're always here, in a way?"

"I suppose so," she nods. "Though I'm not sure why I'm still... lingering. But I have a hunch."

My heart quickens. "What kind of hunch?"

Grandma's eyes meet mine, her gaze intense. "I think it has something to do with helping to find my killer, Lena. As long as you need me, I'm not going anywhere."

I feel a wave of emotions wash over me—relief, gratitude, and a twinge of guilt. Grandma's still here, watching over me, helping me solve her murder. It's comforting to know she's not truly gone, but I can't help feeling at least partly responsible for keeping her tethered to this world.

"Oh, Grandma," I whisper, my voice thick with emotion. "I'm so glad you're here with me. But I hate to think you're stuck because of... because of what happened to you."

She reaches out, her ghostly hand hovering just above mine. "Don't you worry about me, dear. I'm right where I need to be."

Her words strengthen my resolve. I straighten my shoulders, meeting her gaze with determination. "I promise I'll do everything I can to find out what happened to you. Not just for me, but for you too. You deserve to rest, to move on when you're ready."

Grandma's eyes crinkle with pride. "I know you will, Lena. You've always been a fighter."

I nod, feeling a renewed sense of purpose. "We'll figure this out together. And when we do, when the killer is brought to justice, you'll be free to go wherever it is you need to go."

"That's my girl," Grandma says, her form shimmering with what I imagine is approval.

I take a deep breath, my mind already racing with possibilities. "Okay, let's start from the beginning. Tell me everything you remember about that night."

As Grandma begins to speak, I listen intently, determined to catch every detail. I owe it to her to solve this mystery, to give her the peace she deserves. And maybe, just maybe, I'll find some closure for myself along the way.

Chapter 8

I'm clutching the folder of evidence close to my chest as Charlie and I approach the sheriff's office. The weight of Grandma's journal and the threatening notes feels heavy in my hands, but having Charlie by my side gives me strength.

"You ready for this?" Charlie asks, her hand on the door handle.

I nod, steeling myself. "As ready as I'll ever be."

We step inside and Sheriff Mark looks up from his desk, surprise flickering across his face.

"Lena? And Charlie? What brings you two here?"

I stride forward, placing the folder on his desk with a soft thud. "We have evidence, Sheriff. Evidence that my grandmother's death wasn't an accident."

Mark's eyebrows shoot up. He leans back in his chair, crossing his arms. "That's a big claim, Lena. What kind of evidence are we talking about?"

Charlie steps up beside me. "We've got threatening notes and journal entries, Mark. Things that point to foul play."

I open the folder, spreading out the contents. "These notes were found in my grandmother's belongings. They're threatening her, trying to get her to leave the house."

Mark leans forward, his eyes scanning the papers. His brow furrows as he picks up one of the notes. "And you're sure these are related to your grandmother?"

"Absolutely," I say firmly. "And there's more." I flip open Grandma's journal, pointing to the relevant entries. "Look at these. She writes about feeling watched, about strange occurrences around the property. She was scared, Mark."

Charlie nods, adding, "We wouldn't have brought this to you if we didn't think it was serious, Sheriff. You know that."

Mark's eyes dart between us, then back to the evidence. He lets out a long sigh. "I have to admit, this does raise some questions. But it's not conclusive proof of murder."

"No," I agree, "but it's enough to warrant a deeper investigation, isn't it? My grandmother deserves that much."

I watch as Mark's expression shifts from skepticism to concern. He picks up another note, his eyes narrowing as he reads it.

"These threats are pretty specific," he admits, looking up at me. "You're right that this warrants a closer look."

Relief washes over me. "Thank you, Sheriff. That's all we're asking for."

Mark nods slowly, but I can see the hesitation in his eyes. "I appreciate you bringing this to my attention, Lena. But we need to be careful about jumping to conclusions. Threatening notes don't automatically mean murder."

"But they're a start, right?" Charlie chimes in. "It shows someone had it out for her."

"It does," Mark agrees. He leans back in his chair, running a hand through his hair. "Look, I'll open an investigation. We'll look into these threats, see if we can trace where they came from. But I can't promise anything beyond that."

I feel a mix of frustration and hope bubbling up inside me. "What about the journal entries? The way she described feeling watched, the strange occurrences?"

Mark sighs. "It's concerning, I'll give you that. But it's also subjective. We need hard evidence to prove foul play."

"So what's our next step?" I ask, trying to keep the impatience out of my voice.

"I'll assign an officer to look into the threats," Mark says. "We'll also re-examine the scene of your grandmother's death. If there's anything we missed the first time, we'll find it."

Charlie puts a hand on my shoulder. "That's good, right? It's progress."

I nod, but I can't shake the feeling that it's not enough. "And what about us? What can we do to help?"

Mark gives me a stern look. "You two need to be careful. If there is someone behind this, I don't want you putting yourselves in danger. Leave the investigating to us."

I open my mouth to protest, but Charlie squeezes my shoulder. I take a deep breath, trying to calm myself.

"Okay," I say finally. "But please, keep us in the loop. This is my grandmother we're talking about."

Mark's expression softens. "I understand, Lena. I promise we'll do everything we can to get to the bottom of this. Just give us some time to work with what you've brought us."

As Charlie and I gather the documents, ready to leave the sheriff's office, the door bursts open. Annika strides in with Victor close behind, their faces twisted with anger.

"Sheriff Mark, we need to talk about Lena," Annika announces, her eyes narrowing as they land on me.

Victor nods, his gaze cold. "She's caused nothing but trouble since she arrived."

I feel my heart rate spike. "What are you talking about?"

Annika points an accusing finger at me. "You're just here for the inheritance, aren't you? Stirring up all this nonsense about grandma's death."

"That's ridiculous!" I snap, heat rising to my cheeks.

Charlie steps forward, her voice sharp. "How dare you accuse Lena? She loved her grandmother!"

Victor scoffs. "Oh please, none of this murder gossip started until she showed up in town. It's pretty convenient, don't you think?"

"You don't know what you're talking about," I shout, my fists clenching at my sides.

The room erupts into a cacophony of accusations and denials. Annika and Victor's voices rise, trying to drown out Charlie and me as we defend my innocence.

"ENOUGH!" Sheriff Mark's voice booms through the office, silencing us all. He stands, his expression stern. "This stops now. I'm going to get to the bottom of Ingrid's death, but until then, I need everyone to stop pointing fingers and flinging baseless accusations. Is that clear?"

We all nod, chastened by his authoritative tone.

"Good," Mark continues. "Now, I suggest you all go home and let me do my job. And please, try to keep the peace. This town doesn't need any more drama."

As Charlie and I leave the sheriff's office, I can't help but glare at Annika and Victor. Their accusations still ring in my ears, making my blood boil. Charlie places a hand on my back, gently guiding me out the door.

Once we're outside, I take a deep breath of the cool air, trying to calm my racing heart.

"Can you believe them?" I spit out, pacing back and forth on the sidewalk. "How dare they accuse me of... of..."

Charlie steps in front of me, placing her hands on my shoulders to stop my frantic movement. "Hey, hey. Take it easy, Lena. They're just lashing out because they're scared. Don't let them get to you."

I look into his concerned eyes and feel some of the tension leave my body. "You're right. I know you're right. It's just... it's all so frustrating."

"I know," Charlie says, giving my shoulders a gentle squeeze. "Listen, why don't I come over to your place? We could talk, or I could help you clean up a bit. Maybe even make dinner. Anything to help you blow off some steam."

Her offer is tempting, and I'm touched by her thoughtfulness. But the truth is, I'm feeling overwhelmed and in need of some alone time.

"Thanks, Charlie. That's really sweet of you," I say, managing a small smile. "But I think I just need some time to myself right now. To process everything, you know?"

Charlie nods, understanding in her eyes. "Of course. Just remember, I'm here if you need anything. Even if it's just to vent."

"I appreciate that," I say, giving her hand a squeeze. "I'll call you if I need anything, I promise."

As we part ways, I can't help but feel grateful for Charlie's support. But right now, there's only one person I want to talk to—Grandma. I need to tell her about the latest developments in the case, to seek her guidance and comfort.

Chapter 9

The cool evening air does little to calm my nerves as I approach Grandma's house. As soon as I step inside, a chill runs down my spine. Something feels off.

"Grandma?" I call out, my voice echoing through the empty rooms. "Are you here?"

The house creaks and settles, but there's no response. I move through the living room, my eyes scanning for any sign of her ghostly presence. The unease in my stomach grows with each passing moment.

Suddenly, the temperature drops dramatically. I wrap my arms around myself, shivering. A faint shimmer appears in the corner of my eye, and I turn to see Grandma Ingrid's ghost materializing.

"Grandma!" I exclaim, relief flooding through me. But my relief is short-lived as I take in her expression. Her face is etched with worry, her eyes darting around the room as if searching for something.

"Lena," she says, her voice urgent but distant, like a whisper on the wind. "Something's wrong. I can feel it."

I step closer, my heart racing. "What is it, Grandma? What's wrong?"

She shakes her head, frustration clear on her face. "I... I can't see clearly. There's so much fog. But something's coming, Lena. Something bad."

I feel a chill that has nothing to do with her ghostly presence. "What do you mean? Is it about your death? About the investigation?"

Grandma Ingrid's form flickers, like a candle in the wind. "I don't know. I can't... I can't see through the fog. But I feel it, Lena. A darkness approaching."

Her words send a shiver down my spine. I want to ask more, to understand what she means, but her image is already starting to fade.

"Be careful, Lena," she says, her voice growing fainter. "Trust your instincts. And watch out for—"

But before she can finish, she disappears completely, leaving me alone in the suddenly too-quiet house. I stand there, my heart pounding, trying to make sense of her warning.

I stand frozen in the living room, my heart pounding in my chest. Grandma's warning echoes in my mind, and suddenly the shadows in the corners seem longer, more menacing. Every creak of the old house makes me jump.

I can't shake the feeling of dread that's settled over me. With trembling hands, I pull out my phone and dial Charlie's number.

"Hey, Lena, what's up?" Charlie's cheerful voice comes through the speaker.

"Charlie," I whisper, my voice shaky. "I changed my mind. Can you come over? Like, right now?"

There's a pause on the other end. "Lena? Are you okay? You sound scared."

I take a deep breath, trying to steady myself. "I... I just saw Grandma's ghost. She gave me this really ominous warning about something bad coming. I know it sounds crazy, but I'm freaking out here."

"I'm on my way," Charlie says without hesitation. "Lock the doors, okay? I'll be there in five."

True to her word, Charlie arrives in record time. I practically pull her through the door, slamming it shut behind her.

"Whoa, easy there," Charlie says, her eyes wide with concern. "What's going on?"

I quickly recount my encounter with Grandma's ghost, my words tumbling out in a rush. Charlie listens intently, her brow furrowed.

"Okay," she says when I finish. "First things first, let's make sure the house is secure. It'll make you feel better, and it's just good sense anyway."

I nod, grateful for her calm presence. We move through the house methodically, checking every window and door. Charlie tests each lock while I hover nervously behind her.

"This one's a bit loose," she says, jiggling the back door handle. "Got any tools around?"

I fetch Grandma's old toolbox from the hall closet, and Charlie quickly tightens the screws on the lock.

"There," she says, giving the door a firm shake. "That's not going anywhere now."

As we finish our rounds, I feel some of the tension leaving my body. The house feels safer with Charlie here, and with all the entrances secured.

"Thanks for coming," I say, collapsing onto the living room couch. "I know it sounds ridiculous, but after what Grandma said..."

Charlie sits next to me, giving my hand a reassuring squeeze. "Hey, it's not ridiculous. Your grandma's ghost gave you a warning. That's serious stuff. We'll figure this out together, okay?"

I try to focus on the cards in my hand, but my mind keeps drifting back to Grandma's warning. Charlie, bless her, is doing her best to keep things light.

"Got any threes?" she asks, eyebrow raised.

I shake my head. "Go fish."

We play for a while, the familiar rhythm of the game providing a small comfort. But every now and then, I catch myself glancing at the shadows in the corners of the room.

"Hey," Charlie says softly. "Why don't we watch some TV? Might help take our minds off things."

I nod gratefully, and we switch to the couch. Charlie flips through channels until we land on a mindless reality show. The bright colors and petty drama are a welcome distraction.

As the evening wears on, our stomachs start to growl. We raid the kitchen, cobbling together a meal of crackers, cheese, and some canned soup we heat up on the stove. It's not gourmet, but it's warm and filling.

We eat in the living room, the TV still droning on in the background. Despite our best efforts to keep things normal, there's an undercurrent of tension we can't quite shake.

As the clock ticks closer to midnight, exhaustion starts to set in. But the thought of sleeping in separate rooms in this old, creaky house sends a shiver down my spine.

Charlie seems to read my mind. "You know," she says, stifling a yawn, "it might be less scary if we both crash in the living room."

Relief washes over me. "Yeah, that's a good idea. I'll grab some blankets and pillows."

I head to the linen closet, pulling out a mismatched assortment of blankets and pillows. When I return, Charlie's already pushed the coffee table aside to make more floor space.

We set up our makeshift beds, arranging the blankets and pillows into cozy nests on the floor. It reminds me of the sleepovers we used to have as kids, and for a moment, I feel a little better.

"Ready?" Charlie asks, her hand on the light switch.

I take a deep breath and nod. "Ready."

The room plunges into darkness, broken only by the faint glow of streetlights filtering through the curtains. We settle into our blanket piles, the floor hard beneath us in spite of our best efforts.

I lie awake, staring at the ceiling, trying to calm my racing thoughts. Charlie's steady breathing beside me offers some comfort, but I can't shake the feeling that something's off. Suddenly, my nose twitches. I scrunch it, trying to make it stop, but it keeps going like it has a mind of its own.

"Charlie," I whisper, "are you awake?"

No response. I prop myself up on my elbows, scanning the dark room. Nothing seems out of place, but my nose won't stop twitching. It's like my body's trying to warn me of something my mind can't grasp.

Minutes tick by, each one stretching longer than the last. I strain my ears, listening for any unusual sounds, but all I hear is the house settling and the distant hum of traffic.

Then, a soft thud from the back of the house. My heart leaps into my throat.

"Charlie," I hiss, shaking her shoulder. "Wake up!"

She stirs groggily. "Wha-?"

Before I can explain, we hear it—the unmistakable sound of breaking glass. Charlie bolts upright, suddenly wide awake.

"Someone's in the house," I breathe, my voice barely audible, even to my own ears.

We scramble to our feet, tangling in the blankets. Heavy footsteps echo from the kitchen, moving with purpose. Whoever it is, they're not here to steal—they're looking for something. Or someone.

Charlie grabs my hand, pulling me toward the front door. We move as quietly as we can, but my heart is pounding so loud I'm sure the intruder can hear it.

We're almost at the door when a floorboard creaks under my foot. The footsteps in the kitchen stop.

"Run!" Charlie hisses, throwing open the door.

We burst out into the night, the cool air hitting our faces. Harold's house is just next door, and his porch light is my only beacon of hope right now.

We pound on Harold's door, gasping for breath. "Harold! Please, help us!"

I jiggle the door handle, my heart pounding in my chest. To my surprise, it turns easily. The door swings open with a creak that sounds way too loud in the still darkness.

"Come on," I whisper to Charlie, my voice shaking.

We step inside, the darkness enveloping us. The house is eerily quiet, save for the sound of our ragged breathing.

"Harold?" I call out, my hand fumbling along the wall for a light switch. "Harold, are you here?"

My fingers find the switch, and I flick it on. Light floods the entryway, momentarily blinding us. As my eyes adjust, I scan the room, searching for any sign of Harold.

That's when I see it. A dark shape on the floor, just beyond the living room threshold. My stomach drops as I realize what I'm looking at.

"Oh my goodness," Charlie gasps beside me.

Harold lies face-down in a pool of blood, his body unnaturally still. The sight hits me like a physical blow, confirming my worst fears. This isn't a random act of violence. Someone is targeting me, and they're willing to hurt anyone who gets in their way.

I stumble backward, my back hitting the wall. Charlie grabs my arm, steadying me. Her face is pale, eyes wide with shock and fear.

"We need to call the police," she says, her voice barely above a whisper.

I nod, unable to form words. My gaze is locked on Harold's motionless form, my mind reeling. This is my fault. Harold is dead because of me, because of whatever my grandmother was trying to warn me about.

The reality of our situation crashes over me. We're not safe here. We're not safe anywhere. Whoever did this could still be nearby, waiting for us.

Chapter 10

I snap out of my daze, realizing we need to act fast. With shaking hands, I use the phone in Harold's kitchen to call the police station. Charlie stands beside me, her eyes darting between Harold's body and the front door, as if expecting the killer to burst in at any moment.

"Sheriff's office," Mark's gruff voice answers.

"Mark, it's Lena," I say, my voice cracking. "We're at Harold's house, right next door to my grandma—to my house. Harold is... he's dead. Someone broke into my place, and when we ran here for help..."

There's a sharp intake of breath on the other end. "Stay where you are. I'm on my way."

The wait feels like an eternity. Charlie and I huddle by the door, too afraid to venture further into the house. When we finally hear sirens approaching, relief washes over me.

Sheriff Mark bursts through the door, gun drawn. His eyes widen as he takes in the scene.

"Poor old guy," he mutters, holstering his weapon. He turns to us, his face grim. "Are you two okay?"

We nod, still too shaken to speak. Mark calls for backup and starts securing the area. As more officers arrive, he pulls us aside for questioning.

"Tell me everything," he says, his tone serious.

I recount the events of the night, starting with the break-in at my house. Mark listens intently, his brow furrowing deeper with each detail.

"And you didn't see who broke into your place?" he asks.

I shake my head. "No, we ran as soon as we heard them."

Mark sighs, rubbing his forehead. "Look, Lena, I want to believe you. But you have to understand how this looks. You show up in town after years away, start asking questions about your grandmother's death, and now Harold turns up dead."

My stomach drops. "You can't think I had anything to do with this!"

"No, I don't," Mark says quickly. "But the evidence—the circumstantial evidence, anyway—isn't looking good. Your fingerprints are all over the crime scene. You were the last ones to see Harold alive. It's just that I have to follow where the evidence leads, you know?"

"And right now, it all seems to lead straight to me." It isn't a question. I understand how bad this might get. "So what? Are you going to arrest me now?"

Mark's eyes soften, and he shakes his head. "I'm not arresting you tonight, Lena. But I can't ignore the facts staring me in the face either."

I let out a breath I didn't realize I was holding. "So what now?"

"Now," Mark says, leaning in closer, "it would be real helpful if you could start coming up with some evidence that points to someone else. Anyone else."

I blink, trying to process his words. "You want me to... investigate?"

"Not officially," he says, glancing around to make sure no one's listening. "But if you happen to stumble across anything that might shed some light on this mess, I'd sure appreciate it."

Charlie, who's been silent until now, speaks up. "Are you serious? You're asking Lena to play detective when there's a killer on the loose?"

Mark holds up his hands. "I'm not asking her to do anything dangerous. Just... keep your eyes and ears open. Talk to people. You might hear something that could help us crack this case."

I nod slowly, my mind racing. "Okay, I'll see what I can do. But Mark, I need to know something first. Do you really believe I had nothing to do with this?"

He looks me straight in the eye. "I've known you since we were both in school. You might be many things, but a killer ain't one of them. That's why I'm giving you this chance."

His words reassure me, but a nagging doubt remains. "And if I can't find anything? If all the evidence keeps pointing to me?"

Mark's expression turns grim. "Then I'm afraid I'll have no choice but to bring you in. So let's hope it doesn't come to that."

"Yeah, let's hope," I agree. "Before we leave, can you come back to my place with us? We need to check out the break-in there too. And... I'm scared the killer might still be waiting for us."

Mark nods, his hand instinctively moving to his holster. "Of course. Let's go."

As we make our way to the door, something catches my eye. A small, colorful strip of fabric peeks out from under Harold's coffee table. I freeze, my mind racing. It looks so familiar, but I can't quite place where I've seen it before.

"Mark," I call out, pointing to the fabric. "Look at that. Does it seem important?"

He crouches down, examining the strip without touching it. "Could be evidence. Good catch, Lena. I'll have the team bag it up."

He stands, calling over one of the officers to handle the potential clue. As we step out of Harold's house, the cool night air hits my face, and I take a deep breath. The familiar strip of fabric nags at me, like a word on the tip of my tongue that I just can't recall.

We cross the short distance to my grandmother's house—my house now, I remind myself. Mark draws his gun, motioning for Charlie and me to stay behind him as he approaches the front door.

"Stay close," he whispers, pushing the door open slowly.

We enter the darkened house, and I hold my breath, straining to hear any sound that might indicate an intruder. Mark methodically checks each room, his flashlight beam cutting through the shadows. With each cleared space, I feel a mix of relief and mounting tension.

As we reach the kitchen, I notice the broken window and the back door standing slightly ajar. Mark approaches it cautiously, peering out into the yard.

"Looks like they're long gone," he says, turning back to us. "But we'll dust for prints, see if we can find anything. I'll have a patrol car drive by regularly tonight, but you two need to be extra careful. Lock all the doors and windows, and don't hesitate to call if anything seems off."

Charlie nods, her face pale in the dim light. "What if the killer comes back? Should we stay somewhere else?"

"That might not be a bad idea," Mark agrees. "I seriously doubt the perp will come back tonight, but I don't want you to stay here if it makes you uncomfortable."

I shudder at the thought. "You really think we'll be safe here for the night? Like, you're confident they won't come back?"

Mark's expression softens. "It's unlikely, but we can't rule it out. Just stay alert and do whatever your gut says, okay?"

We walk Mark to the front door, and I'm struck by the scene outside. In the short time we've been inside, a crowd has started gathering on the street. Neighbors in hastily thrown-on robes and slippers stand in small clusters, whispering and pointing.

As we step onto the porch, I spot two familiar faces pushing their way to the front of the growing crowd.

Annika and Victor.

Because of course the night wasn't already bad enough.

I freeze on the porch as Annika's shrill voice cuts through the murmur of the crowd.

"There she is!" Annika shouts, jabbing a finger in my direction. "I told you all, didn't I? It can't be a coincidence!"

My heart races as every eye turns to me. Victor stands beside Annika, his face a mask of righteous anger.

"She's murdered poor Harold now, too!" Annika continues, her voice rising with each word. "First our grandmother, and now this? How many more people have to die before you do something, Sheriff?"

Mark steps forward, holding up his hands in a placating gesture. "Now, hold on a minute—"

But Annika isn't finished. She pushes past the neighbors, marching right up to the edge of my yard. "You have to arrest her immediately! It's the only way to keep the rest of us safe!"

Murmurs of agreement ripple through the crowd. I feel my face burning with a mix of shame and anger. Charlie grabs my arm, as if afraid I might bolt.

"You don't know what you're talking about," I manage to say, but my voice sounds weak even to my own ears.

Victor joins in, his eyes boring into mine. "We all knew something wasn't right when you came back to town, asking all those questions. Now look what's happened."

Mark steps between us, his voice firm. "That's enough, both of you. This is an ongoing investigation, and I won't have you throwing around baseless accusations."

"Baseless?" Annika scoffs. "She was the last one to see Harold alive! Her fingerprints are probably all over his house!"

I flinch at her words, knowing they're true. Mark notices and shoots me a warning glance.

"I understand you're all scared," he says, addressing the crowd. "But I need everyone to go back to their homes now. We'll release more information as soon as we can."

Annika shakes her head vehemently. "That's not good enough, Sheriff!" she shouts, her voice cutting through the night air. "We want to see this menace taken off our streets. Now!"

The murmuring in the crowd grows louder, a rising tide of fear and anger. I feel like I'm drowning in it, unable to catch my breath.

Mark turns to me, his expression grim. He leans in close, speaking quietly so only I can hear. "Lena, I might need you to come down to the station. For your own safety, if nothing else."

My heart races, panic clawing at my chest. This can't be happening. I'm about to protest when something catches my eye.

It's subtle, almost imperceptible, but it's there. And suddenly, everything clicks into place.

I take a deep breath, steadying myself. "Sheriff," I say, loud enough for the crowd to hear, "I think you really should make an arrest tonight."

Mark's eyebrows shoot up in surprise. The crowd falls silent, waiting.

"But," I continue, my voice growing stronger, "it shouldn't be me."

Chapter 11

I take a deep breath, trying to calm my racing heart. Mark gives me a pleading look, his eyes intense.

"This had better be good, Lena. For your sake," he says under his breath.

I nod, feeling the weight of the moment. "I just need a minute," I reply, my voice barely above a whisper. Then, turning to Charlie, I say, "Can you run back to Harold's and collect that scrap of evidence we found earlier?"

Her eyes widen in understanding. Without a word, she darts off, disappearing into the darkness.

The crowd murmurs, restless and impatient. I can feel their eyes on me, judging, accusing. Annika's glare burns into me, her arms crossed tightly over her chest. Victor stands beside her, his face a mask of righteous anger.

I take another deep breath, trying to steady myself. My mind races, piecing together the clues we've gathered. I know I'm right about this, but doubt gnaws at the edges of my certainty. What if I'm wrong? What if this backfires spectacularly?

The seconds tick by agonizingly slow as we wait for Charlie to return. Mark shifts his weight from foot to foot, clearly uncomfortable with the tension in the air. I can tell he's torn between his duty as sheriff and his desire to protect me.

"Lena," he says quietly, "if you've got something, now's the time."

I give a quick nod and begin, my voice shaky at first but growing steadier as I speak.

"The night I arrived at my grandmother's house, something strange happened. A rock shattered the window, and in the chaos, I caught a whiff of something... something sweet and floral. It was so distinct, but I almost forgot about it until recently."

The crowd's murmurs die down as they lean in to listen. Even Annika's glare softens slightly, replaced by a flicker of curiosity.

"I found an entry in my grandmother's journal," I continue, my heart racing. "She wrote about a sweet smell in the air shortly before she died. I didn't think much of it at the time, but then..."

I turn to face Annika, our eyes locking. "When I visited you, Annika, that same floral scent was in the air at your house. It hit me like a ton of bricks."

Annika's face pales, her arms dropping to her sides. Victor shifts uncomfortably beside her.

Mark steps closer, his brow furrowed. "What are you saying, Lena?"

"I'm saying that this scent might be a key piece of evidence. It was present at two significant moments—the night someone tried to scare me away and in my grandmother's final days. And now, it's lingering around Annika's home."

The crowd buzzes with renewed interest. I can see the gears turning in Mark's head as he processes this information.

A few feet away, Annika's face contorts with anger, her pale skin flushing red. She takes a step forward, her hands clenched into fists at her sides.

"This is absolutely ridiculous!" she shouts, her voice echoing through the tense silence. "A smell? You're basing your accusations on a smell?"

The crowd starts to murmur again, some nodding in agreement with Annika. I feel my confidence wavering, but I stand my ground.

Annika continues, her voice dripping with disdain, "You can't use a smell as evidence. It's absurd! And even if you could, who is everyone going to believe?"

She turns to address the crowd, her arms spread wide. "Let's not forget all the suspicious evidence pointing to Lena. The timing of her arrival, her sudden inheritance, her lack of an alibi. Are we really going to ignore all that because of some supposed floral scent?"

I open my mouth to respond, but Sheriff Mark beats me to it. He steps forward, his voice calm but authoritative.

"Circumstantial evidence," he corrects, looking directly at Annika. "And what Lena's presenting is also circumstantial evidence. It may not be conclusive on its own, it's certainly worth investigating further. That is, if you expect me to investigate the circumstantial evidence against Lena, too."

Annika scoffs, crossing her arms again. "Circumstantial or not, it's hardly enough to clear her name. If anything, this wild goose chase just makes her look more desperate."

I nod slowly, my nose twitching as I catch another whiff of that sweet, floral scent. "You're right, Annika. A scent alone isn't much to go on. But there's another piece of evidence I'd like you to explain."

Annika's eyes narrow, her posture stiffening. "I don't know what you're talking about."

Just then, Charlie comes racing back, her breath coming in short gasps. She holds up a small evidence bag, triumphant despite her exhaustion.

"I got it, Lena!" she pants, handing the bag to me.

I take it, my heart pounding as I hold it up for everyone to see. Inside is a small scrap of colorful fabric, its pattern unmistakable. My eyes dart from the fabric to Annika's shirt, and I watch as recognition dawns on the faces of those around us.

The pattern matches Annika's shirt perfectly.

A hush falls over the crowd as all eyes turn to Annika. Her face, already pale, now drains of what little color it had left. She takes an involuntary step back, her hands clutching at the hem of her shirt.

"Where..." she starts, her voice barely above a whisper. She clears her throat and tries again, louder this time. "Where did you get that?"

I hold the evidence bag a little higher, making sure everyone can see it clearly. "This was found at the scene of Harold's death. Care to explain how a piece of your shirt ended up there, Annika?"

The crowd's murmurs grow louder, and I can see Mark's posture change as he shifts into full sheriff mode. His eyes are fixed on Annika, watching her every move.

Annika's gaze darts around, looking for an escape, but she's surrounded. Victor stands beside her, his face a mask of shock and confusion. He takes a small step away from her, and I can see the hurt in his eyes as he looks at the woman he thought he knew.

"I... I don't..." Annika stammers, her usual confidence crumbling. "That could be anyone's shirt. It's a common pattern."

But even as she says it, we all know it's a lie. The pattern is unique, a custom design that Annika often boasted about.

I've heard her mention more than once how she had it specially made.

I watch as Sheriff Mark's eyes narrow, his gaze fixed on Annika. He takes a step forward, his voice calm but firm.

"Annika, I'm going to need you to take off your coat and let me inspect your shirt."

Annika's eyes widen, a flicker of panic crossing her face. She wraps her arms tightly around herself, shaking her head.

"This is ridiculous," she sputters. "You can't just—"

Mark cuts her off, his tone leaving no room for argument. "We can do this the easy way right here, or we can do it the hard way down at the station. Your choice."

The crowd around us falls silent, the tension palpable. I hold my breath, my heart racing as I watch Annika's internal struggle play out on her face.

Finally, with a frustrated growl, she shrugs off her coat. "Fine," she grumbles, her voice dripping with venom. "But this doesn't mean anything."

As she pulls off her coat, I catch a glimpse of her sleeve. My breath catches in my throat. There, on the fabric of her shirt, is a jagged tear—right where the piece in the evidence bag would fit.

Mark steps closer, inspecting the rip. "Annika," he says slowly, "I'm afraid you're going to have to come down to the station with me."

For a moment, Annika stands frozen, her eyes darting between Mark and me. Then, without warning, she lunges forward, her hands outstretched and reaching for my throat.

I barely have time to react, stumbling backward as I try to avoid her grasp. But before she can reach me, Mark steps between us, his broad shoulders blocking Annika's path.

"That's enough!" he shouts, grabbing Annika's arms and pulling them behind her back.

The crowd around us murmurs in shock, struggling to process what they've just witnessed as Mark places a pair of handcuffs around Annika's wrists. I take a deep breath, steadying myself before I speak.

"It's no mystery why she killed our grandmother," I say, my voice carrying over the whispers. "She wanted that house—badly. And not just to live in it."

I turn to face Victor, who's staring at Annika with a mix of horror and disbelief. "She wanted to sell it to you, didn't she, Victor? The developer who has been eyeing that prime piece of land for years."

Victor's eyes widen, and he takes a step back, shaking his head. "I... I had no idea," he stammers.

"Of course you didn't," I continue. "Annika played us all. When Grandma wouldn't cut her in on the will, she took matters into her own hands. She couldn't stand the thought of me inheriting everything while she got nothing."

The crowd gasps, and I can see the realization dawning on their faces. Annika struggles against Mark's grip, but he holds her firmly.

"But there's still one thing I don't understand," I say, my brow furrowing. I turn to face Annika directly. "Why Harold? What did that poor old man ever do to deserve what happened to him?"

Annika's face twists into a snarl, her eyes burning with hatred. For a moment, I think she's going to lunge at me again, but Mark's grip tightens, holding her back.

"He knew!" she spits out, her voice filled with venom. "That nosy old fool figured it out. He was going to tell you everything!"

I feel a chill run down my spine as the pieces fall into place. Harold, always so kind and observant, must have noticed something was off. And Annika couldn't risk him exposing her plan.

"So you silenced him," I say softly, the weight of it all settling on my shoulders. "Just like you tried to silence me."

I stand there, stunned, as Annika's rage boils over. Her face contorts with fury, and she starts shouting, her words echoing through the night air.

"I should have gotten away with it!" she screams, struggling against Mark's grip. "It was perfect! I had everything planned out!"

Her eyes lock onto mine, blazing with hatred. "But you," she spits, "you kept stumbling onto clues. It's like you were being led by the hand! How did you keep figuring things out?"

I feel a chill run down my spine at her words. It's true that I've had some lucky breaks, but I never thought...

"I would have had it all," Annika continues, her voice cracking. "The house, the money, everything. And no one would have suspected a thing if it weren't for you and your meddling!"

Mark starts to lead her away, but she keeps ranting over her shoulder. "You don't deserve any of it! I'm the one who deserves a lucky break! I'm the one who should have inherited everything!"

As Mark guides her towards his patrol car, her voice fades into the distance. The crowd around us starts to disperse, murmuring amongst themselves about what they've just witnessed.

I take a deep breath, trying to process everything that's happened. That's when I see it—a flicker of movement at the edge of my vision. I turn, and my heart skips a beat.

There, just a few feet away, stands the ghostly figure of my grandmother. She's smiling at me, her eyes twinkling with pride and love.

"Charlie," I whisper, a similar smile spreading across my own face. "Do you see her?"

Charlie looks at me, confused. "See who?"

I gesture toward where my grandmother's ghost is standing, but Charlie just shakes her head.

"There's no one there, Lena," she says gently. Then, after a pause, she adds, "But I bet Ingrid is at peace now, right? You solved the mystery and caught her killer. She must be so proud of you."

I nod, my eyes still fixed on the spot where I saw my grandmother. As I watch, her figure slowly fades away, but her smile lingers in my mind.

"Yeah," I say softly. "I think she is."

Chapter 12

I stand on the front porch of my grandmother's—no, my house—watching the sun dip below the horizon. It's been a few weeks since that fateful night when Annika's plot unraveled, and the dust has finally started to settle.

The old house creaks and sighs around me, but it no longer feels eerie or threatening. Instead, it's comforting, like a warm embrace from the past. I've spent the last few weeks cleaning, sorting through old belongings, and making the place my own. It's a delicate balance—honoring Grandma Ingrid's memory while carving out a space for myself.

I take a sip of tea from my favorite mug—one of Grandma's that I've claimed as my own—and breathe in the crisp evening air. The garden is coming along nicely. I've pulled out the weeds and planted some new flowers. It's therapeutic, getting my hands dirty and watching new life spring from the earth.

Charlie drops by often, sometimes with a casserole or a batch of cookies. We sit on this very porch, talking about everything and nothing. She's been a rock through all of this, and I'm grateful for her friendship.

Inside, I've set up a small writing nook in what used to be Grandma's sewing room. The antique desk faces the window, giving me a perfect view of the garden. It's where I've started working on my novel—a mystery, of course. Who would have thought that solving a real-life murder would spark my creativity?

As I stand lost in thought, a familiar sensation runs down my spine. I turn, and there she is—Grandma Ingrid's ghost, shimmering in the fading light.

"Lena, my dear," she says, her voice like a whisper on the wind.

My heart skips a beat. "Grandma? I thought... I thought you were gone."

She smiles, her ethereal form glowing softly. "I couldn't leave without saying goodbye properly."

I step closer, fighting the urge to reach out and touch her. "I've missed you."

"And I've missed you, sweetheart. But I'm so proud of you. You solved the mystery, you set things right."

Tears prick at my eyes. "I couldn't have done it without you."

Grandma Ingrid shakes her head. "You did it, Lena. Your strength, your intelligence, your persistence—that was all you."

I look around at the house, the garden, everything I've been working on. "I hope I'm doing right by you, by your memory."

"Oh, darling," she says, her eyes sparkling with unshed tears. "You're doing more than right. You're making this place your own, just as I always hoped you would."

A lump forms in my throat. "I wish you could stay."

She reaches out, and though I can't feel her touch, I swear I sense a warmth on my cheek. "I'll always be with you, Lena. In your heart, in your memories, in every corner of this house."

I nod, unable to speak.

"You've got a bright future ahead of you," Grandma continues. "That novel you're writing? It's going to be wonderful. And Charlie? She's a good friend."

I laugh through my tears. "Always looking out for me, aren't you?"

"Always," she agrees. "But now, it's time for me to go. Remember, Lena, I love you. I'm so proud of the woman you've become."

I watch as Grandma Ingrid's form begins to fade, her edges blurring into the twilight. My heart aches, but I force a smile, determined to be strong for her. We both know this is goodbye.

"I love you too, Grandma," I whisper, my voice thick with emotion.

She smiles one last time, and I close my eyes, waiting for the moment when I'll feel her presence disappear completely. Seconds tick by, then minutes. The air around me remains charged with an otherworldly energy.

I open my eyes, expecting to find myself alone on the porch. But to my shock, Grandma Ingrid is still there, looking just as surprised as I feel.

"Grandma?" I gasp. "You're still here?"

She furrows her brow, glancing down at her translucent hands. "I... I don't understand. I was ready to move on. I said my goodbyes."

I take a tentative step closer. "Maybe there's something still keeping you here? Something unfinished?"

Grandma shakes her head, bewildered. "No, dear. I made my peace. The mystery's solved, the truth is out, and you're settling into the house. There's nothing left for me to do."

We stand in silence for a moment, both of us at a loss. The porch creaks beneath my feet, and a cool breeze rustles through the garden, but Grandma's form remains unaffected, hovering just inches above the wooden planks.

"Well," I say, trying to inject some levity into the situation, "I guess you're stuck with me for a little while longer."

Grandma Ingrid chuckles, but I can see the concern in her eyes. "It seems so, my dear. Though I can't imagine why."

I stand on the porch, my mind racing as I try to make sense of this unexpected turn of events. Grandma Ingrid's ghostly form shimmers in the fading light, her brow furrowed in concentration.

"Lena, dear," she says, her voice tinged with uncertainty. "I can't help but wonder if there's something we've overlooked."

I lean against the porch railing, my tea forgotten in my hand. "What do you mean, Grandma?"

She paces back and forth, her feet never quite touching the wooden planks. "Well, we solved the mystery of my death, that's true. But perhaps there's something else, something deeper that needs addressing."

"Like what?" I ask, my curiosity piqued.

Grandma Ingrid pauses, her translucent form glowing softly in the twilight. "I'm not entirely sure, but I have a feeling it might be connected to the town's history. There are secrets around here that go back generations."

I straighten up, my heart quickening. "What kind of secrets?"

"Oh, all sorts," she says, waving a spectral hand. "Old feuds, buried treasures, unsolved disappearances. This town has seen its fair share of mysteries over the years."

"And you think one of these old secrets might be keeping you here?"

Grandma nods slowly. "It's possible. I've always felt a strong connection to this place, to its past. Maybe there's something left unresolved, something that needs to be brought to light."

I can't help but feel a mix of excitement and apprehension. "So, what do we do? How do we figure out which mystery needs solving?"

A mischievous glint appears in Grandma's eyes. "Well, my dear, I think that's where you come in. You've proven yourself quite the detective. Perhaps it's time for you to dig a little deeper into our New Oslo's colorful history."

The weight of uncertainty settles on my shoulders, but it's not as heavy as I expected. Grandma Ingrid's presence, even in this ghostly form, brings a strange comfort.

"Well," I say, turning to face her, "I guess we're in for another adventure, huh?"

Grandma's eyes twinkle with that familiar mischievous glint. "It seems so, my dear. Though I must admit, I hadn't planned on haunting you for quite this long."

I can't help but laugh. "I don't mind, Grandma. In fact, I'm kind of glad you're sticking around."

And I mean it. The thought of diving into another mystery should terrify me after everything we've been through, but instead, I feel a spark of excitement. Maybe it's because I know I won't be facing it alone.

"So, where do we start?" I ask, my mind already racing with possibilities. "The library? Town records?"

Grandma Ingrid nods approvingly. "Those are good places to begin. But don't forget, Lena, sometimes the best stories are passed down through generations. Talk to the old-timers, listen to their tales. You might be surprised at what you uncover."

I nod, already making mental notes. The future stretches out before me, a blank canvas waiting to be filled. It's daunting, but also exhilarating. I may not know exactly what's coming, but I do know one thing: I'm not alone.

"You know," I say, smiling at Grandma, "I'm actually looking forward to this. It's nice knowing you'll be around for a while longer, even if we're not sure why."

Grandma's form shimmers, and for a moment, I swear I can feel the warmth of her embrace. "Oh, my dear Lena. I'm glad too. We make quite the team, don't we?"

I nod, feeling a surge of affection for this stubborn, wonderful ghost. Whatever mystery lies ahead, whatever secrets New Oslo is hiding, I know we'll face it together. And somehow, that makes the unknown future seem a little less daunting and a lot more exciting.

Get *Granny's Ghost and the Poisoned Punch* HERE[1]!

---

1. https://www.amazon.com/gp/product/B0DGNN9QNK

Also by Sloane Finley

Death by Dessert Series
Death by Chocolate Cupcake[2]
Death by Devil's Food Cake[3]

Ghostly Gumshoe Series
Granny's Ghost and the Haunted Homicide[4]
Granny's Ghost and the Poisoned Punch[5]
Granny's Ghost and the Bake-Off Bribe[6]
Granny's Ghost and the Deadly Dinner Party[7]
Granny's Ghost and the Movie Night Murder[8]
Granny's Ghost and the Murdered Medium[9]
Granny's Ghost and the Basement Burial[10]
Granny's Ghost and the Murdered Magician[11]
Granny's Ghost and the Deadly Delphinium[12]
Granny's Ghost and the Killer Caroler[13]

2. https://www.amazon.com/Death-Chocolate-Cupcake-Dessert-Mystery-ebook/dp/
B0DPGS8S8Z

3. https://www.amazon.com/gp/product/B0DR7GTS38

4. https://www.amazon.com/gp/product/B0DFZR8LV6

5. https://www.amazon.com/gp/product/B0DGNN9QNK

6. https://www.amazon.com/gp/product/B0DHB1CBQL

7. https://www.amazon.com/gp/product/B0DJ7PW47X

8. https://www.amazon.com/gp/product/B0DJQ4R3L1

9. https://www.amazon.com/gp/product/B0DKB6Y47K

10. https://www.amazon.com/gp/product/B0DL3GRP97

11. https://www.amazon.com/gp/product/B0DLVJJJ33

12. https://www.amazon.com/gp/product/B0DMYJ5RQ6

Granny's Ghost and the Fatal Fashion Show[14]
Granny's Ghost and the Cook-Off Killer[15]
Ghostly Gumshoe Collection (Books 1 - 3)[16]

Fur-ensic Files Series
Fetch Me a Felon[17]
Best in Show, Worst in Murder[18]
Dachshund Dynasty[19]
Fur-ensic Files Complete Collection (Books 1 - 3)[20]

---

13. https://www.amazon.com/gp/product/B0DNY9H8YM

14. https://www.amazon.com/gp/product/B0DQHXXW7Z

15. https://www.amazon.com/gp/product/B0DRWFBDK4

16. https://www.amazon.com/Ghostly-Gumshoe-Collection-Paranormal-Mystery-ebook/dp/B0DHPDBYQ9

17. https://www.amazon.com/gp/product/B0DFVQMWV5

18. https://www.amazon.com/gp/product/B0DHPWBRFT

19. https://www.amazon.com/gp/product/B0DJG9KWYL

20. https://www.amazon.com/Fur-ensic-Files-Collection-Sloane-Finley-ebook/dp/B0DJZV9ZLZ